Bats are the only mammals that can really fly,
and flight has made them very successful.
There are more than nine hundred species, living in
almost every habitat from subarctic tundra to
tropical forests and deserts. Birds may rule the air
by day, but bats are the monarchs of the night.

This book is about one of the pipistrelle bats.
Pipistrelles are found around the world,
from North America to Africa, Europe,
Asia and Australia.

For Henry Venner Woodcock and his big brothers,
Alfie and Thomas
N.D.

For Ailsa
S.F-D

First published 2001 by Walker Books Ltd
87 Vauxhall Walk, London SE11 5HJ

This edition published 2015

2 4 6 8 10 9 7 5 3

Text © 2001 Nicola Davies
Illustrations © 2001 Sarah Fox-Davies

This book was typeset in Cochin and Sanvito

Printed in China

British Library Cataloguing in Publication Data:
a catalogue record for this book is available
from the British Library

ISBN 978-1-4063-6701-0

www.walker.co.uk

BAT LOVES THE NIGHT

Nicola Davies

illustrated by

Sarah Fox-Davies

WALKER BOOKS

AND SUBSIDIARIES

LONDON · BOSTON · SYDNEY · AUCKLAND

Bat is waking,
upside down as usual,
hanging by her toenails.

Her beady eyes open.
Her pixie ears twitch.

She shakes her
thistledown fur.

She unfurls her wings,
made of skin so fine the finger bones
inside show through.

*This pipistrelle bat
is no bigger than
your thumb.*

*A bat's wing is its
arm and hand.
Four extra-long fingers
support the skin of the wing.*

Bats' toes are shaped like hooks,
so it's no effort for a bat to hang
upside down.

Now she unhooks her toes
and drops into black space.
With a sound like a tiny umbrella
opening, she flaps her wings.

Bat is flying.

Out!

Out under the broken tile
into the night-time garden.

Over bushes, under trees,
between fence posts,
through the tangled hedge
she swoops untouched.
Bat is at home in the darkness,
as a fish is in the water.
She doesn't need to see –
she can hear where she is going.

Bats can see. But in the dark, good ears
are more useful than eyes.

Bat shouts as she flies, louder than
a hammer blow, higher than a squeak.
She beams her voice around her like a
torch, and the echoes come singing back.
They carry a sound-picture of all
her voice has touched.
Listening hard, Bat can hear every
detail, the smallest twigs, the
shape of leaves.

*Using sound to find your way like this
is called echolocation.
Some bats shout through their mouth,
and some shout through their nose.*

Gliding and fluttering
back and forth,
she shouts her torch of
sound amongst the trees,
listening for her supper.

All is still...

15

Then a fat moth takes flight below her.

Bat plunges, fast as blinking, and grabs it in her open mouth.

But the moth's pearly scales are moon-dust slippery. It slithers from between her teeth.

Bat dives, nets it with a wing tip, scoops it to her mouth.

This time she bites hard.
Its wings fall away, like the
wrapper from a toffee.
In a moment the moth is eaten.
Bat sneezes.
The dusty scales got up her nose.

Hunting time has run out.
The dark will soon be gone.
In the east the sky is getting light.
It's past Bat's bedtime.

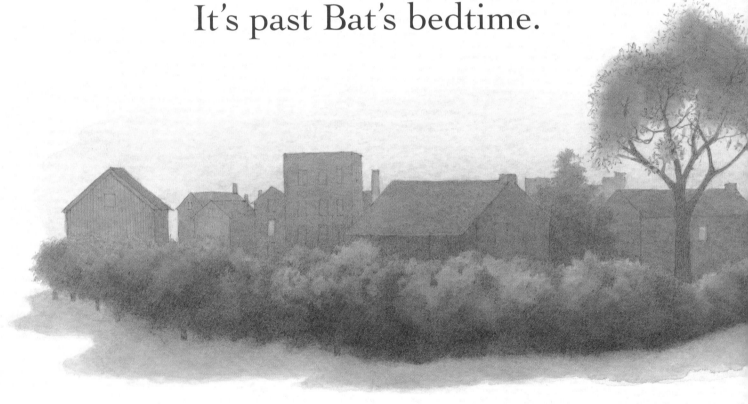

The place where bats sleep in the day is called a roost.
It can be in a building, a cave, or a tree, so long as it's dry and safe.

She flies to the roof in the last shadows,
and swoops in under the broken tile.

Inside there are squeakings.
Fifty hungry batlings hang in a huddle,
hooked to a rafter by outsized feet.
Bat lands and pushes in amongst them,
toes first, upside down again.

Baby bats can't fly.
Sometimes mother bats carry their babies when
they go out, but mostly the babies stay behind in the roost
and crowd together to keep warm.

Bat knows her
baby's voice, and
calls to it.

The velvet scrap
batling climbs aboard
and clings to her fur
by its coat-hanger feet.

Wrapped in her
leather wings,
it suckles
Bat's milk.

Baby bats drink mother's milk until
they learn to fly at a few weeks old.
Then they can leave the roost
at night to find their own food.

Outside the birds are singing.
The flowers turn their faces to the sun.
But inside the roof hole,
the darkness stays.
Bat dozes with her batling,
waiting.

Bats are nocturnal. That means they rest by day
and come out at night to search for food.

When the tide of night rises again
Bat will wake, and plunge
into the blackness, shouting.

Bat loves the night.

Index

Look up the pages to find
out about all these batty things.
Don't forget to look at both
kinds of word –
this kind and
this kind.

Mexican freetail bat
(Tadarida brasiliensis)

About the Author

Nicola Davies is a zoologist and has studied all kinds of mammals, from whales in the Indian Ocean and Newfoundland to bats in west Wales. She is also the acclaimed author of many books for children, including the Nature Storybooks *Big Blue Whale*, *One Tiny Turtle*, *I (Don't) Like Snakes*, *Just Ducks!* and *White Owl, Barn Owl*.

About the Illustrator

Sarah Fox-Davies has illustrated many picture books for children, including *Walk with a Wolf* by Janni Howker, which was shortlisted for the Kurt Maschler Award and Highly Commended for the Times Educational Supplement Junior Information Book of the Year Award; and *Little Beaver and the Echo* by Amy MacDonald, which was shorlisted for the Children's Book Award.

Note to Parents

Sharing books with children is one of the best ways to help them learn. And it's one of the best ways they learn to read, too.

Nature Storybooks are beautifully illustrated, award-winning information picture books whose focus on animals has a strong appeal for children. They can be read as stories, revisited and enjoyed again and again, inviting children to become excited about a subject, to think and discover, and to want to find out more.

Each book is an adventure into the real world that broadens children's experience and develops their curiosity and understanding – and that's the best kind of learning there is.

Note to Teachers

Nature Storybooks provide memorable reading experiences for children in Key Stages 1 and 2 (Years 1–4), and also offer many learning opportunities for exploring a topic through words and pictures.

By working with the stories, either individually or together, children can respond to the animal world through a variety of activities, including drawing and painting, role play, talking and writing.

The books provide a rich starting-point for further research and for developing children's knowledge of information genres.

Nature Storybooks support the literacy curriculum in a variety of ways, providing:
- a focus for a whole class topic
- high-quality texts for guided reading
- a resource for the class read-aloud programme
- information texts for the class and school library for developing children's individual reading interests

Find more information on how to use Nature Storybooks in the classroom at
www.walker.co.uk/naturestorybooks
Nature Storybooks support KS 1–2 English and KS 1–2 Science